# NONNA TELL ME A STORY

*Lidia's Christmas Kitchen*

# NONNA TELL ME A STORY

## Lidia's Christmas Kitchen

### LIDIA BASTIANICH

Illustrated by Laura Logan

RP|KIDS
PHILADELPHIA • LONDON

To Olivia, Lorenzo, Miles, Ethan, and Julia, I proudly dedicate this book to you. With much love, I share this real story of my childhood with you and with it, the wonderful memories that grace each page. I also dedicate this book to children all around the world who need to know, to learn, to be cognizant, and in control of, the food they ingest as they grow into adulthood.

The one message I wish to convey to every child of the world is a simple one, deeply important, and hopefully one that they can come to appreciate. May their food be healthy and grown in harmony with the earth and its seasons. May it be respected and not be wasted to ensure enough supply for the world's future generations of children. And lastly, and perhaps most importantly, may it provide a source of nourishment, pleasure, and communication at every family's table.

—Lidia Bastianich

9  8  7  6  5  4  3  2  1
Digit on the right indicates the number of this printing

Library of Congress Control Number: 2010923801
ISBN 978-0-7624-3692-7

Cover and interior design by Frances J. Soo Ping Chow
Edited by Kelli Chipponeri
Typography: Perpetua, Murray Hill, and Univers

Published by Running Press Kids,
an imprint of Running Press Book Publishers
2300 Chestnut Street
Philadelphia, PA 19103-4371

Visit us on the web!
www.runningpress.com
www.lidiasitaly.com

Dear Reader,

The holidays are all about family, food, and love. It is a time to come together and share the best things about the season and ourselves. Some of my fondest memories are of my family at Christmastime as a young girl growing up in Istria. We did not have much then; most everything we ate, we grew or made ourselves. The simple delights of family, cooking, and working together, brought great satisfaction to me then, and still do.

Nowadays I spend the holidays in the United States, where I came as a young immigrant at age 12, with my own children and grandchildren. They call me Nonni, (a form of Nonna) an endearing way of calling me "Grandma" in Italian. I enjoy sharing my Italian traditions with them, and creating new ones together in America.

Wherever your family comes from, whether privileged or less fortunate, I am sure there are special holiday traditions that you honor each year. I hope what I share in this book will encourage you and your family to celebrate, and bring simple heartfelt warmth into your own holidays. Perhaps you will discover a favorite recipe or two, and start a new tradition of baking or cooking them together each year.

In carrying out your unique traditions, may you appreciate the traditions of others as well, so together we may encourage communal values for all humanity. May this holiday season bring love and peace to your home, and to everyone around the world.

Merry Christmas and *Buon Natale*,

"One-two-three-four-five," Nonni Lidia counted. "Olivia, Lorenzo, Miles, Ethan, and Julia. The gang's all here!"

"Ahem!" a voice said. "Aren't you forgetting *someone*?" It was Nonna Mima, great-grandmother Erminia, joking as she joined the group.

"Mamma," Nonni Lidia said. "I could never forget you!"

"Don't forget Lucia, either," Julia said with a giggle, as she held up her doll.
"And Miss Lucia, of course!" Nonni Lidia added.

"What are we going to do today, Nonni?" Miles asked.

"Well," Nonni Lidia said. "While your parents are out Christmas shopping, I thought maybe we could make some cookies and decorate my tree. I just got it a few days ago. Come see."

In the living room, Lorenzo looked the tree over carefully. "You picked a good one, Nonni," he said. "We'll have to do an extra-special job decorating it."

"I think you're right, Lorenzo," Nonni Lidia said. "You know, when I was a girl we didn't have a big tree like this from a store. No. Just a small juniper bush from the woods."

"How did you fit all of your presents under a little bush?" Ethan asked.

"We didn't have so many presents then," Nonni Lidia said. "Just small things—fruits, nuts, sweets. Christmas was more about being together. That was what mattered most."

"Tell us the story of Christmases when you were a girl, Nonni," Olivia said.

"Yes! Tell us," all the children chimed in.

"Well," Nonni Lidia began. "We always spent Christmas at my grandparents' home. It was my favorite place—a magical place. Their town had only thirty houses, along one road.

My grandparents' house was set around a courtyard. And my, that courtyard was a whole world in itself!"

"At one end, near the pine trees, there was Nonna Rosa's smokehouse with its blackened walls. She prepared food out there, delicious sausages, ham, and bacon. Garlic, onions, and great bouquets of fragrant bay leaves were hung on the wall to dry. Nonna Rosa even cooked for the pigs there too—potato peels, pumpkins, table scraps—nothing went to waste."

"There were pigs?" Miles asked.

"Oh yes," Nonni Lidia said. "And chickens and goats and rabbits and geese, too. "

"The rabbits were my favorite. I used to love playing with the baby bunnies. They were so soft and fuzzy. But the geese were loud and always poking at me with their beaks. I liked them best roasted for Christmas dinner!"

"But what about Christmas?!" Ethan said.

"Right!" Nonni Lidia said. "Back to the story.... Before each Christmas, while we played in the woods, my brother Franco and I would scout out the best juniper bush for our Christmas tree. Usually just a little seedling. We'd tell our grandfather, and he would go back and get the exact one.

"I can still see the juniper branches, full of deep green needles with small frosty-blue berries. And the smell! Like a pine tree but better—sweet and spicy and fresh."

"We always put the tree in the kitchen and covered the bottom with fresh moss that Franco and I would gather outside. The warmth from the kitchen fire would spread the smell of juniper all through the house. Sometimes it mixed with the smell of orange peels that Nonna Rosa left drying on the stove to make tea later."

"What did you put on your tree, Nonni?" Julia asked.

"Ahh, that was the best part," Nonni Lidia said. "We were very creative. We made decorations ourselves. And even better, most of them were edible! There were cookies made from *pignoli*, pine nuts. Franco and I would gather the pine cones ourselves. The tiny nuts were just inside."

"We'd also make little wreaths from dried figs and bay leaves, stringing them one by one. And we'd tie fresh fruit to the tree. Delicious tangerines, small apples, and sickle pears, all with the stems still on."

"With the cookies, and candies, and fruits, and wreaths, our tree was truly something to see…and smell…and best of all, *taste*!"

"Speaking of Christmas trees," Nonni Lidia said. "I think it's time we decorate this one. What do you say?"

Nonni Lidia, Nonna Mima, and the children began opening the boxes of ornaments. There were glass balls, and glittery snowflakes, and colored lights. The store-bought decorations were pretty, but something didn't feel quite right.

"These ornaments don't feel special enough," said Lorenzo.

"Yeah," said Ethan. "These are boring!"

"We could put tangerines on the tree," suggested Miles.

"And little fig wreaths," said Olivia.

"And cookies!" Julia squealed. "Lucia loves cookies!"

In no time, everyone got to work...
Olivia and Lorenzo found figs and bay leaves to make wreaths.

Nonna Mima helped Julia measure flour for the cookies.

Ethan grabbed tangerines from the fruit
bowl, while Miles found some ribbon.

And Nonni Lidia, she watched it all
with a big happy smile.

Soon the whole house was filled with delicious smells. There were cookies baking and nuts roasting. The scent of cinnamon, orange, and nutmeg danced through the air.

Nonni Lidia closed her eyes. "Mmmm," she said. "Now *that* smells like Christmas."

While everyone was still busy working, Lorenzo pulled Nonni Lidia to the side.

"Nonni," he whispered. "Do you think you'll ever have a Christmas as special as the ones you had as a little girl?"

Nonni Lidia looked around the kitchen, then gave Lorenzo a wink. "You know what," she said. "I think I just might."

That year, the whole family agreed Nonni Lidia's tree was the best ever. And everyone had an extra special *new* old-fashioned Christmas—especially Nonni Lidia!

# Recipes

# Fruit Tea (Compote)

Yield: 2 quarts

3 pounds apples

2 quarts water

1 medium lemon

¼ pound prunes, or more to taste

½ cup sugar or to taste

1. Rinse and core the apples; slice them into thick wedges, with peel. Put the apples and water in the pot and set over medium high heat. Peel the lemon—zest only—and add to the compote; squeeze in the juice of the lemon, too. Drop in the prunes and stir in the ½ cup sugar.

2. Bring the compote to the boil, cover the pot and reduce the heat to maintain a gentle bubbling simmer. Cook slowly until compote is reduced somewhat in volume for about half an hour or more.

3. Strain through a colander or large sieve and either reserve the cooked fruit to eat or press the pulp gently to release the juices. Taste and sweeten with sugar if you like. Enjoy the beverage warm or hot as tea on cold days or chilled in warmer days.

# "Ugly But Good" Cookies (Brutti ma Buoni)

Yield: 4 dozen cookies

8 large egg whites

Pinch of salt

2 cups confectioners' sugar, sifted

2 cups shelled hazelnuts, toasted, skinned, and coarsely chopped

1. Preheat the oven to 275°F. Line 2 baking sheets with parchment paper. Beat the egg whites and salt in a bowl with an electric mixer with the whisk attachment until foamy. Continue beating, adding the sugar gradually, until all the sugar is incorporated and the egg whites hold stiff and shiny peaks.

2. Scrape the beaten whites into a wide, heavy saucepan and set over medium-low heat. Stir in the hazelnuts and cook, stirring constantly, until the batter comes away from the sides of the pan and is light golden brown, about 20 minutes. (The batter will deflate quite a bit as it cooks.)

3. Remove the pan from the heat. Drop the batter by rounded teaspoonfuls onto the prepared pans. Bake until golden brown and firm to the touch, about 30 minutes. Remove and cool completely before serving. Store at room temperature in an airtight container for up to 1 week.

# COOKIE CRUMBLES
## (FREGOLATA)

Yield: two 9-inch cookies, serves 12

2 tablespoons (¼ stick) soft
   unsalted butter, for the pans

1 cup plus 3 tablespoons
   all-purpose flour

1 scant cup sugar

¼ teaspoon salt

1¼ cups whole unblanched
   almonds, toasted

3 large egg yolks

½ cup mini chocolate chips

6 tablespoons heavy cream,
   plus more if needed

1. Preheat the oven to 350°F. Assemble two (9-inch) springform pans and butter the bottom disks and about an inch up the sides.

2. Chop the almonds coarsely into chunks the size of chocolate chips. Stir the flour, sugar, and salt together in a mixing bowl and toss in the chopped almonds. Beat the yolks together briefly and drizzle over the dry ingredients. Toss with a fork to blend. Add the chocolate chips and toss some more until they are all incorporated. Drizzle the cream over by tablespoons, tossing and stirring to moisten the nut mixture evenly. It should be crumbly but not floury; add a small amount of more cream if necessary.

3. Pour half of the crumb mixture into each buttered cake pan. Spread and press the crumbs down lightly in an even thick layer covering the bottom of the pan. Bake about 25 minutes or until the cookie rounds are nicely browned and starting to shrink from the side ring of the pan. Let them cool on a rack about 20 minutes and then remove the springform side rings and bottom disk. It is easier to remove the cookies from the base of the springform if they are still slightly warm, but not hot.

4. Serving the fregolata is fun, smack the fregolata in the center with the back of a spoon; it will crumble in many pieces and you can eat the crumbs. It is delicious soaked in milk or for Mom and Dad, serve with a cup of espresso. Serve as a garnish with poached fruits or ice cream.

# FRIED RIBBON COOKIES (CROSTOLI)

Yield: 3½ dozen cookies

6 tablespoons (¾ stick)
  very soft unsalted butter

⅓ cup sugar

½ teaspoon salt

¼ cup milk

1 large egg

1 large egg yolk

3 tablespoons orange juice

1½ tablespoons fresh lemon juice

Finely grated zest of a lemon, about
  2 teaspoons

Finely grated zest of an orange,
  about 2 tablespoons

2½ cups all-purpose flour, plus
  more for rolling the dough

6 to 8 cups vegetable oil for
  frying, or as needed

¼ cup confectioners' sugar,
  or as needed

1. Blend butter, sugar, and salt in the food processor. Add milk, egg and yolk, citrus juices and citrus zests and process everything together until smooth. Scrape down the sides of the bowl, dump in all of the flour, and process in pulses until the dough comes together. Clean the bowl again and pulse a few more times to mix thoroughly.

2. Scrape the dough out onto a lightly floured work surface and knead briefly into a soft smooth ball. If it is sticky, knead in more flour in small amounts. Wrap the dough tightly in plastic and chill for 30 minutes to 1 hour. (You can keep it refrigerated up to 1 day but let it return to room temperature before rolling.)

3. Cut the chilled dough in half and work with one piece at a time. Flatten the dough on a lightly floured work surface and roll it out to a rough square shape, approximately 16 inches on a side. Trim the edges of the square and with a fluted cutter, divide it into 10 strips, about 1½ inches wide. Cut across all the strips in the middle to form 20 ribbons, each about 7 inches long (though they shrink after you cut them). One at a time, tie each ribbon into a simple overhand knot. (When tying the crostoli, leave the knot very loose so there will be a gap for tying a ribbon for hanging once they are fried.) If necessary, stretch the ends gently so they're long enough to knot. Place the knotted crostoli on a sheet pan lined with parchment or wax paper, leaving room between them so they don't stick to each other. Roll out the second piece of dough; cut and tie the same way.

**4.** Meanwhile, pour vegetable oil in the pan to a depth of 2 inches. Set over medium heat to gradually reach frying temperature. When you're ready to start frying, raise the heat and test the oil by dropping in a scrap piece of dough: the fat should bubble actively around the dough, but it shouldn't get dark quickly. (If you have a frying thermometer, heat the oil to 350°F. And be sure to use long handled tools, hot pads, and caution when deep frying.)

**5.** Using long-handled tongs, quickly drop the first batch of crostoli into the fryer—raise the heat to return the oil to the frying temperature. Don't crowd the cookies—fry only 10 or 12 at a time in a 10-inch diameter pan. The cookies will first drop to the bottom but will soon float to the surface. Turn them frequently with tongs and a spider or slotted spoon, to cook evenly.

**6.** Fry the crostoli for 4 minutes or so, as they color gradually to dark gold. Adjust the heat as needed to maintain the oil temperature and prevent rapid browning. When crisp and golden all over, lift them from the oil with a spider or spoon, drain off the oil, then lay them on layers of paper towels to cool. Fry the remaining crostoli in batches the same way. Store in a sealed cookie tin or plastic container and keep them dry. To serve, pile the crostoli on a serving plate in a heaping mound. Put the confectioners' sugar in a small mesh sieve and dust generously over the cookies.

# Pine Nut Cookies
## (Amaretti con Pignoli)

Yield: Makes 3 dozen cookies

1 pound canned almond paste
1½ cups sugar
3 large egg whites
1 cup pine nuts (optional)
¼ cup confectioners' sugar,
  or as needed (optional)

**1.** Arrange one rack in the upper third of the oven and the other in the lower third. Preheat the oven to 350°F. Line 2 baking sheets with parchment paper.

**2.** Crumble the almond paste into a mixing bowl. Beat with a handheld electric mixer until finely crumbled. Sprinkle the sugar over the almond paste and continue to beat until the sugar is incorporated. Beat in the egg whites, one at a time and continue beating until the batter is smooth.

**3.** If using the pine nuts, spread them out on a plate. Pinch off a tablespoon-size piece of dough and roll between your palms to form a ball. Roll the ball in pine nuts or just place it on the baking sheet if you want plain cookies. Repeat with the remaining dough.

**4.** Bake the cookies until lightly browned and soft and springy, about 20 minutes. Remove and cool completely on wire racks before serving. The cookies can be stored at room temperature for up to 1 week and are delicious with or without pine nuts.

**Note:** The plain cookies can also be dusted with confectioners' sugar before serving.

# SESAME COOKIES
## (BISCOTTI AI SEMI DI SESAMO)

Yield: 4 dozen cookies

1 cup sesame seeds (or sprinkles)
2 large eggs
1 teaspoon pure vanilla extract
½ teaspoon salt
1 cup all-purpose flour
1 cup semolina flour
⅔ cup sugar
1½ teaspoons baking powder
Pinch of ground nutmeg
½ cup (1 stick) unsalted butter,
   at room temperature

**1.** Arrange one oven rack in the upper third of the oven and the other in the lower third. Preheat the oven to 350°F. Spread the sesame seeds out on a baking sheet and bake them on the lower rack until toasted to golden brown, about 8 to 10 minutes. Shake the pan once or twice as they bake so they toast evenly. Line 2 baking sheets with parchment paper.

**2.** In a large bowl, whisk the eggs, vanilla, and salt until blended. Stir the all-purpose flour, semolina flour, sugar, baking powder, and nutmeg together in a mixing bowl until blended. With your fingers, work the butter into the flour mixture until the butter resembles small cornflakes. Pour in the egg mixture and mix well into a dough. Cover and refrigerate the dough for at least 30 minutes to let it firm up.

**3.** Lightly flour your hands and pinch off a nectarine-size piece of the dough and roll it out with the palm and fingers of your hands, using light pressure, to a rope about ½ inch in diameter. Cut the rope into 2-inch lengths and roll them in the sesame seeds or sprinkles to coat completely. Transfer the coated cookies to the prepared baking sheets and repeat with the remaining dough and seeds.

**4.** Bake the cookies until golden brown, about 15 to 17 minutes. Rotate the baking sheets from rack to rack and side to side once during baking so the cookies bake and brown evenly.

# FRUIT JAM OR CHOCOLATE TARTLET COOKIES (CROSTATA)

Yield: 2½ dozen cookies

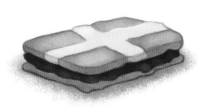

### Dough

3 cups all-purpose flour

½ cup sugar

1 teaspoon baking powder

1 cup (2 sticks) cold unsalted butter, cut into small pieces

2 large egg yolks

¼ cup ice water, or as needed

### Chocolate Layer

5 ounces semisweet chocolate

3 tablespoons heavy cream

### Chocolate Filling

⅔ cup sugar

6 tablespoons (¾ stick) soft unsalted butter

2 large eggs

1 tablespoon all-purpose flour

⅓ cup shelled hazelnuts, toasted, and skinned

Grated zest of 1 orange

3 ounces semisweet chocolate, chopped

### Optional Filling

1½ cups chunky apricot, cherry, peach, or plum preserves

1. To make the dough, stir the flour, sugar, and baking powder together in a mixing bowl. Drop in the butter and toss to coat it with the flour mixture. Using the tips of your fingers, rub the butter into the flour until the pieces of butter resemble small cornflakes. Work quickly to keep the butter as firm as possible. Beat the egg yolks and ¼ cup ice water in a separate bowl until blended. Drizzle over the flour-butter mixture and toss just until you have a rough dough, adding another teaspoon or so of water to get the dough to come together, if necessary. Don't overmix. Turn out onto a work surface and knead lightly a few times, just to gather the dough into a ball. Wrap the dough tightly in plastic wrap and refrigerate for at least 1 hour or up to 1 day.

2. Preheat the oven to 350°F. For the chocolate layer, melt chocolate and cream together in a double boiler. For the main chocolate filling, put sugar and butter in a food processor. Process until smooth. Add eggs and process again until smooth. Add flour, nuts, zest, and chocolate and process in short pulses to combine. You still want small chunks of nuts and chocolate.

3. Cut off two-thirds of the dough and roll into a rectangle. Fit the dough in a 9-by-13-inch baking pan, pressing it about half an inch up the sides. Spread the warm chocolate layer on the bottom of the crust. Chill it for a few minutes to set the chocolate a bit and then spread the main filling over to cover the chocolate. Roll out the remaining dough into a rectangle. Cut the dough into ½-inch strips. Form a lattice pattern over the filling with the strips of dough by arranging half of them perpendicularly over the filling. Bake until the dough is golden brown, about 25 minutes. Remove and cool completely before cutting it into squares. Crostata cookies can be stored in an airtight container at room temperature for up to 5 days.

**Note:** Instead of the chocolate layer and filling, you can also just spread the crust with your favorite jam.

# Chocolate Chip Oatmeal Cookies

Yield: 4½ dozen cookies

2½ cups all-purpose flour

2 cups quick-cooking oatmeal (not instant)

1½ teaspoons baking soda

1 teaspoon salt

1 cup (2 sticks) unsalted butter, melted and cooled slightly

1½ cups packed light brown sugar

1 cup sugar

3 large eggs, lightly beaten

1½ teaspoons pure vanilla extract

1 (12-ounce) package semisweet chocolate chips

1. Preheat the oven to 350°F and arrange a rack in the top and bottom thirds of the oven. Line 2 large baking sheets with parchment.

2. Whisk together flour, oatmeal, baking soda, and salt in a bowl.

3. In a large bowl, beat butter and sugars with an electric mixer at high speed until pale and fluffy, about 2 to 3 minutes. Slowly add eggs, beating until creamy, about 1 minute. Beat in vanilla. Reduce speed to low and mix in flour mixture until just blended and then stir in chips with a wooden spoon. Cover dough and refrigerate for 30 minutes to 1 hour to firm up.

4. Scoop dough in 2 tablespoon portions and roll into balls. Arrange them 2 to 3 inches apart on baking sheets as the cookies will spread quite a bit.

5. Bake 2 pans of cookies at a time, until golden, about 14 to 15 minutes, rotating the pans from the top to bottom racks halfway through baking. Cool on wire racks.

**Note:** To hang these cookies, let them cool completely and then punch a hole in the middle of the cookie with a drinking straw. Loop a thin piece of ribbon through the hole.

# Peanut Butter and Jelly Cookies

Yield: 5 dozen cookies

3 cups all-purpose flour

1 teaspoon baking powder

½ teaspoon salt

1 cup (2 sticks) unsalted butter,
at room temperature

1 cup creamy peanut butter

1 cup packed light brown sugar

1 cup sugar, plus more for
rolling the cookies

2 large eggs

1 cup grape jelly

1. Mix flour, baking powder, and salt in a bowl. In a separate bowl, using an electric mixer, beat butter, peanut butter, and both sugars until light and fluffy.

2. Mix in half of the flour mixture, then beat in the eggs one at a time. Beat in remaining flour mixture just until a soft dough forms. Cover the bowl with plastic wrap and refrigerate for 1 hour, to firm up the dough.

3. Preheat the oven to 350°F. Line 2 large baking sheets with parchment paper. Spread about a cup of sugar on a plate. For each cookie, roll 1 heaping tablespoonful of dough into a ball, then roll the ball in the sugar. Arrange the dough balls 2½ inches apart on prepared baking sheets.

4. Bake until puffed but still soft, about 8 minutes. Remove baking sheets from oven and carefully make a small crater in the middle of each cookie using a teaspoon-size measuring spoon. Fill each crater with ¼ to ½ teaspoon grape jelly. Bake cookies until they are golden brown on the bottom and edges, about 8 minutes more. Cool the cookies on baking sheets for 5 minutes, then transfer the cookies to racks and cool completely. (These cookies can be prepared up to 3 days ahead. Store in an airtight container at room temperature.)

# Angel Food Cupcakes

Yield: 1 dozen cupcakes

½ cup cake flour
⅔ cup sugar, divided
Pinch of salt
5 large egg whites,
　at room temperature
½ teaspoon cream of tartar
1 teaspoon pure vanilla extract

**Glaze**
½ cup confectioners' sugar
Juice of ½ lemon
Grated lemon zest, for garnish

1. Preheat the oven to 375°F. Line a cupcake pan with paper liners. In a medium bowl, stir together the cake flour, ⅓ cup sugar, and the salt.

2. In an electric mixer with the whisk attachment, beat egg whites and cream of tartar to soft peaks. With the mixer at medium speed, gradually add the remaining ⅓ cup sugar. Beat at high speed to stiff, glossy peaks. Lower speed and mix in vanilla. Fold in the flour mixture in 3 additions, taking care to deflate the batter as little as possible. Divide the batter among the muffin tins and smooth out the tops.

3. Bake until the tops are golden. When you insert a toothpick in the center of a cupcake, it should come out clean, about 5 minutes. Cool on a wire rack for 5 minutes and then remove the cupcakes from the tin to cool completely.

4. When the cupcakes are completely cool, make the glaze. In a small bowl, stir together the confectioners' sugar and lemon juice to make a thick glaze. Drizzle the glaze over the tops of the cupcakes and garnish with lemon zest. Let the glaze harden before serving.

# SIMPLE SUGAR COOKIES

Yield: 4 dozen (2-inch) cookies

3 cups all-purpose flour
1 teaspoon baking powder
Pinch of salt
1 cup (2 sticks) unsalted butter,
　　at room temperature
1 cup sugar
1 large egg
1 teaspoon pure vanilla extract

1. Sift flour, baking powder, and salt together. In an electric mixer fitted with the paddle attachment, beat together butter and sugar until light and fluffy. Add egg and vanilla and mix well. Add flour mixture and mix until just combined. It might be a bit crumbly, but it will come together when chilled. Divide the dough into 4 equal parts, shape into 4 disks, wrap with plastic wrap and refrigerate about 1 hour or more, until firm.

2. Preheat the oven to 350°F. Line 2 baking sheets with parchment and arrange racks in the top and bottom third of the oven. Roll out the dough between 2 sheets of parchment to about ⅛ inch thick. Cut out circles with a 2-inch round cookie cutter and place them on the baking sheets. Use a 1-inch round cutter to cut out the centers and make "O" shapes that can be hung on the tree. Decorate with colored sanding sugar. Bake for 8 to 9 minutes or until the edges are golden. Remove the cookies from the oven, let them cool on baking sheets for 5 minutes, and then transfer them to a wire rack.

**Note:** These cookies can also be baked plain and then decorated with the same royal icing from the Chocolate Star Cookies recipe on the following spread.

# ALMOND APRICOT BUTTER COOKIES

Yield: 4 dozen cookies

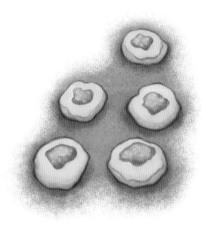

2½ cups all-purpose flour
½ teaspoon salt
1 cup (2 sticks) unsalted butter,
   softened
1 cup sugar
1 large egg
½ teaspoon pure vanilla extract
½ teaspoon almond extract
⅓ cup apricot preserves
⅓ cup slivered almonds, toasted

1. In a bowl, whisk together flour and salt. Beat butter and sugar with an electric mixer until very pale and fluffy, about 4 minutes, then beat in egg and both extracts. At low speed, mix in flour mixture just until a dough forms. Wrap the dough in plastic and chill until firm, about 1 hour.

2. Preheat the oven to 350°F with racks in the top and bottom thirds. Line 2 large baking sheets with parchment paper. Pinch off heaping teaspoon-size balls of dough and roll into balls. Place the balls on the prepared baking sheets, about 2 inches apart and flatten them slightly with the palm of your hand. Bake them until they are puffed, but not browned, about 8 minutes.

3. Remove the baking sheets from the oven and carefully make a small crater in the middle of each cookie using a teaspoon-size measuring spoon. Fill each crater with ¼ to ½ teaspoon of preserves and sprinkle a couple of slivered almonds in the preserves. Continue to bake the cookies until they are golden brown on the bottom and edges, about 8 minutes more. Cool the cookies on baking sheets for 5 minutes and then transfer them to racks and cool completely. (These cookies can be prepared up to 3 days ahead. Store in an airtight container at room temperature.)

# ALMOND STUFFED FIGS

Yield: 2 dozen

1 cup pomegranate juice
Juice of 1 large lemon,
    freshly squeezed (about
    3 tablespoons)
½ cup plus 1 tablespoon sugar
1 cup chopped toasted almonds
1 cup chopped toasted
    walnut halves
¼ cup honey
⅓ cup cocoa powder
¼ teaspoon ground cinnamon
¼ teaspoon ground cloves
1 pound whole dried figs

**1.** Arrange a rack in the middle of the oven, and heat to 350°F. Pour the pomegranate juice, lemon juice, and ½ cup sugar into the baking dish, and whisk together until the sugar dissolves. For the stuffing, put the chopped nuts in a bowl, pour in the honey, and stir well so all the nuts are coated. Sprinkle on the cocoa powder, cinnamon, cloves, and the last tablespoon sugar; stir and toss until thoroughly distributed.

**2.** With a sharp knife, slice into each fig from top to bottom—following the line of the stem—splitting it, but leaving the split halves still attached. Fold open each fig like a book, exposing the cut surfaces, and top each half with a spoonful of the nut stuffing. Press the stuffing into the fruit interior, so it sticks and stays, then place the open fig in the baking dish, with the stuffing on top, resting in the juice on the bottom. Stuff all the figs this way, and arrange them in the dish.

**3.** Tent the baking dish with a sheet of aluminum foil, arching it so it doesn't touch the stuffing, and pressing it against the sides. Bake the figs for 20 minutes, until the juice is bubbling and the figs are softened, then remove the foil, and bake another 35 to 40 minutes, basting the figs two or three times with the juice, until the figs are caramelized and tender and the juice has reduced to a syrup. Let the figs cool in the baking dish for at least 5 minutes before serving warm, or leave them to serve later at room temperature. Put three or four figs for each serving on a dessert plate or in a bowl, and drizzle over them some of the pan syrup.

**Note:** They are delicious served warm over vanilla ice cream.

# CHOCOLATE STAR COOKIES

Yield: 4 dozen cookies

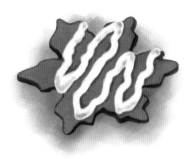

2 cups all-purpose flour
½ cup unsweetened Dutch-
   processed cocoa powder
½ teaspoon baking powder
½ teaspoon salt
1 cup (2 sticks) unsalted butter,
   softened
¾ cup sugar
1 large egg yolk
1 teaspoon pure vanilla extract
Equipment: 2- or 3-inch fluted star
   or snowflake cookie cutter

1. Whisk together flour, cocoa powder, baking powder, and salt. Beat butter and sugar with an electric mixer until pale and fluffy about 2 minutes, then beat in yolk and vanilla. On low speed, mix in flour mixture just until a dough forms. Divide the dough in half, flatten each piece into a disc and then chill them, wrapped in plastic wrap, until firm, for 2 to 3 hours.

2. Preheat the oven to 350°F with racks in top and bottom thirds. Line 2 baking sheets with parchment paper. Roll out 1 piece of dough between the sheets of parchment paper into a 14-by-10-inch rectangle (⅛ inch thick). Cut out as many stars as possible, reserving and chilling scraps, then quickly transfer the cookies to the baking sheet, arranging them ½ inch apart. (If the dough becomes too soft, return it to the freezer until it is firm.)

3. Bake it until it is firm and slightly puffed, about 10 minutes. Cool the cookies on the baking sheet for 5 minutes, then transfer them to the rack to cool completely. (The cookies will crisp as they cool.) Make more cookies with the remaining dough and scraps, rerolling scraps only once.

**Note:** If you want to hang these cookies on the tree, use a drinking straw to punch a hole through the cut cookies before baking.

# ROYAL ICING
# TO DECORATE COOKIES

1 large egg white
Pinch of cream of tartar
2 cups confectioners' sugar
Sprinkles, sanding sugar
   or nonpareils, for decorating
Equipment: A disposable pastry
   bag with a small round tip

1. In an electric mixer with the whisk attachment, beat egg white and cream of tartar until foamy. Sift in half of the sugar and beat until smooth, about 1 to 2 minutes. With the mixer running, gradually add the remaining sugar and beat on high speed until the icing is smooth and thick. The icing should be thick, but not too thick to be pressed through a pastry bag. Adjust the consistency with more confectioners' sugar or water.

2. Transfer the icing to a pastry bag with a small round tip. Pipe decorations of your choice, adding each one before the icing hardens.

# PALACINKES

Yield: 2 dozen small crepes

2 large eggs

2 cups milk

½ cup club soda

¼ cup sugar

¼ teaspoon salt

1 teaspoon vanilla extract

2¼ cups all-purpose flour

6 tablespoons (¾ stick) melted
   butter, cooled slightly

Grated zest of 1 lemon

Grated zest of 1 orange

1 tablespoon vegetable oil,
   for frying

**For serving:**

Melted semisweet chocolate,
apricot jam, confectioners' sugar,
whipped cream, fresh berries,
chopped walnuts

1. In a bowl, whisk the eggs. Add the milk, club soda, sugar, salt, and vanilla. Whisk well until the sugar has dissolved. Gradually sift the flour to form a batter about the thickness of heavy cream. Stir in the melted butter and the citrus zests.

2. In a 6- or 7-inch nonstick pan, heat 1 tablespoon vegetable oil over a moderately high flame, pouring off the excess. Tilt the heated and oiled pan at a 45 degree angle to the floor and pour in a scant ¼ cup batter at the top. Twist your wrist in a circle and allow the batter to cover the bottom of the pan in an even layer.

3. Return the pan to the heat, reduce the heat to medium, and cook the crêpe until lightly browned, 45 seconds to 1 minute. Flip it carefully with a spatula and cook the second side until brown spots appear, another 30 seconds or so. Flip the crêpe onto a plate and repeat with the remaining batter, lightly brushing the pan with oil as needed.

4. The crêpes can be served rolled or folded in quarters. Fill with melted chocolate and walnuts or apricot jam. Fold and top with confectioners' sugar, whipped cream, berries, or walnuts.

## DECORATING THE TREE

When I was a little girl, we didn't go to the store to buy our Christmas decorations—we would make them. First, we would have to harvest all of our supplies. We would head off to the cantina, or cellar, where a year's worth of goodies such as walnuts, almonds, figs, apricots, prunes, and raisins would be stored to dry—the very best of these were always saved for holiday decorating. Seasonal fruits and cinnamon sticks were also gathered, and freshly baked Christmas cookies doubled as both ornaments and sweet treats for snacking. Throughout the year, we would save ribbons so that when it was time to decorate our tree, we would have an abundance of beautifully colored strands to tie our ornaments. When you decorate your Christmas tree with these homemade ornaments, hang the heaviest ones toward the center of your tree—near the trunk—as not to weigh down the branches.

One of our holiday traditions was to decorate our tree with seasonal fruits, such as lady apples and sickle pears. We tied them with a ribbon from the stem and hung them directly on the tree branches. We also wrapped tangerines like little Christmas packages. You can make these too. Simply lay the ribbon flat on a table and place the tangerine directly in the center. Bring each side of the ribbon up toward the top of the tangerine, and make a firm knot. Leave about 2 to 3 inches of ribbon strand on each end to make a loop. Take another small piece of ribbon and thread it through the loop and tie it into a bow. Hang the tangerine by its loop on the branch of your tree. Be sure to alternate between the fruits throughout your tree, and remember to hang the heaviest ornaments toward the inside.

My family also saved walnuts and almonds, which we wrapped in colored foils saved throughout the year from our caramel treats. Once wrapped, the nuts reminded me of little candies with their twisted ends. Sometimes when it was a meager year, we substituted perfectly round pebbles that we collected at the seashore for the nuts. My brother and I would use this pebble trick after we had snuck candies from our tree and needed to find something to replace them with—it worked every time!

We baked cookies and goodies and hung them on the ends of the branches. The edible ornaments were always my favorites! For every cookie that hung from our tree, there was a missing cookie that found its way to either my brother's tummy or mine. For those treats that made it to our tree, we slipped colored ribbons through each center and hung them directly on our tree.

We decorated with fig and bay leaf wreaths, which were another favorite of mine. There was always an opportunity to find a fig that was not compact enough for the wreath and sneak it into my mouth. When you make your own fig and bay leaf wreaths, be sure to buy plump figs, a mixture of regular golden and black Mission figs will do. Have some fresh bay leaves ready—dry bay leaves are fine, but they crack easily. Using lanyard or fishing line and a big tapestry needle, begin threading the figs and bay leaves together. Alternate between one fig and one bay leaf. To make a lightweight wreath, create one that is no more than 4 inches in diameter. To hang this yummy wreath from your tree, thread a ribbon through the center hole. Leave a large loop of ribbon on top and hang it from a sturdy branch.

By the time my brother and I made the apricot and prune towers, our tummies were full, but the towers still managed to have a few missing pieces of fruit—we couldn't help ourselves. Each tower was made up of two apricots and two prunes—alternated and stacked, one on top of the other. To make your own towers, simply thread the fruit together with a large tapestry needle and fishing line or lanyard. But first, tie a big knot at the bottom, stack the fruit, and finally tie a bow on top, leaving a loop so that the finished tower can be hung on a branch.

For a finishing touch to our tree, we hung cinnamon sticks. I fondly remember their fragrant aroma, which filled the air. All you need to do is to take a strand of ribbon, tie it tightly around one end of the stick, and make a knot. Keeping about 3 inches of ribbon on each side, make a bow and hang the cinnamon stick from the loop.

Once all the ornaments hung from our tree, we would take first aid cotton, pulled in thin strips, and spread it out on each branch to resemble snow. After a long day of decorating, we would gather around our tree and enjoy a warm glass of Nonna Rosa's homemade fruit compote. Not only did this sweet drink warm us before bedtime, but its fragrance, which permeated the house as we fell off to sleep, was filled with the spirit of the holiday season.